2011

For Ophelia,
    forever

THIS BOOK BELONGS TO

<u>TRISTAN DANIELS</u>

Hello.
I hope you have fun in our little
corner of the world!
Very soon, you will meet Softi,
Tally, Robosofti and all their
friends as they learn about our
wonderful world.
So until we meet again, look around.
The world is yours.

Lavinia

Copyright 2002 by Lavinia Branca Snyder.

A LAVINIA'S WORLD™ book in the **Softi's Adventures**™ series.
Lavinia's World and Softi's Adventures are trademarks of Lavinia Branca Snyder.
Published by Aurora Libris Corp., New York. All rights reserved.
Printed in China

Library of Congress Catalog Number: 2003104533
ISBN 1-932233-35-0

Text edited by Pam Pollack
Special thanks to Frank Palminteri,
and, as always, thank you Brian for being both my husband and my friend.

Softi's Adventures
Mission In Space

Story by Lavinia Branca Snyder
Illustrations by Lavinia Branca Snyder,
Nevena Christi, and Yevgeniya Yeretskaya

Published by Aurora Libris Corp., New York

One September afternoon Tally was in her bedroom with her friends Softi the hamster and Robosofti the robot hamster. They were playing and looking at Softi's space stamp collection. Softi had been interested in space since Tally gave him his first moon rock.

"The universe is so big," said Tally. "I've read that there are millions of stars and planets in it. I'm sure we'll learn cool stuff about space in Miss Ariza's class."

"If I win the contest I'll learn a lot of cool stuff about space too," said Softi.

"What contest did you enter this time?" asked Tally with a smile. Softi was always entering contests.

"The winner of this contest will get to be the first hamster to go into outer space."

"Cool," said Robosofti.

"Let's go out and look at the sky through Tally's telescope," Softi Said.

The stars were just coming out over the Smithers' house. The three friends were taking turns looking at the planets through Tally's telescope. Suddenly Robosofti's radio whiskers began to hum. "Hey, I'm getting a transmission from someone named Professor Puzzlepop. It's a message for you, Softi."

Softi's ears perked up with interest. "What is he saying?" Softi asked eagerly.

"He says he wants to see you at the World Space Agency first thing tomorrow morning."

"Oh boy," said Softi, "I bet this is about the space hamster contest."

Early the next morning Tally, Softi and Robosofti bicycled over to the World Space Agency. Robosofti climbed on top of Softi and they put on Mr. Smithers' overcoat. To get past the security guard downstairs, the three friends pretended to be Dr. Little and his daughter.

"Aah, right on time," said Professor Puzzlepop when they came into his office. "Well done, Softi. You won the contest."

"How did you know it was me?" asked Softi.

"Well, you had an appointment, didn't you? We're sending you to Europa, one of the moons of Jupiter. We think on this moon we may discover whether there's other life in the universe. We want you to collect moon rocks. You'll start your space training immediately."

"Wow," said Softi. "I'm the happiest hamster in the universe."

For the next three weeks Softi spent every moment in training. He was really happy when he got a space suit made just for him. He learned how to put it on and float around in the antigravity chamber. He ate special dried food, even dried ice cream - it was crinkly, not creamy, but still delicious. He discovered that you can't open a box of milk in the zero gravity of space because the milk will come right out.

Every night Softi sent a radio transmission that Robosofti could pick up on his whiskers. Softi told his friends about all the cool space stuff he was doing.

After talking to Softi, Tally would fall asleep and dream about going into space herself.

The night before takeoff Softi called Tally and Robosofti to say goodbye.

"Good luck in space," Robosofti said.

"Be careful and take your vitamins," Tally said.

"I'll do my best to make you proud, guys," Softi told them.

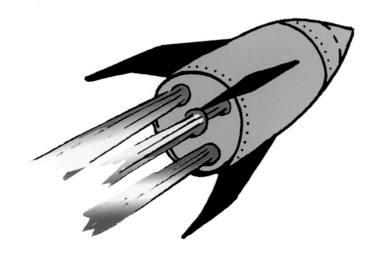

The next morning Softi climbed up into the rocket and strapped himself in. He put on his big round helmet, which looked like a fish bowl. Ten, nine, eight, seven, six, five, four, three, two, one - lift off.

Before he knew it he was streaking through space surrounded by twinkling stars. Weeks went by. He passed the Hubble Telescope and saw Saturn and Venus before Europa finally appeared from behind the rim of Jupiter.

"Gosh, it's beautiful," said Softi. "I'm sure one lucky hamster."

Softi called Mission Control on the interstellar radio. "You can see millions of stars from up here. They're so beautiful and bright."

"Softi, our sensors indicate that you should be in visual range of Europa," Mission Control said.

"Yes, I see it now," Softi exclaimed. He was looking down at the moon's surface. It looked like a crinkled up piece of paper. He activated his retrorockets and the rocket landed with a skip and a bounce.

Softi put on his airpack and went out to dig. Clink, clink, clink, clink.

"These are neat rocks," he said and put them in his bucket. He had the odd feeling he was being watched, but that's silly, he thought. Who could be watching him here?

But Softi was right. Somebody was watching him from behind a big rock.

It was an alien named Eposh. He was a little smaller than Softi. I wonder why he's so interested in rocks, thought Eposh. Oh, he must live in that thing over there. He sneaked closer to have a good look at the rocket.

Softi took his samples back to the rocket but didn't notice Eposh follow him in.

"Softi to Mission Control," he called. "Message for Professor Puzzlepop: Mission accomplished. I'm coming home."

"Great job, Softi. See you soon," replied Mission Control.

Softi blasted off and pointed the rocket toward Earth. Meanwhile Eposh had started exploring the inside of the rocket's living quarters - the sleeping bag, the potty, the food storage locker. It was all very interesting, but Eposh was getting hungry so he decided to have some lunch. He ate a cheese and veggie pattie and then he ate the freeze-dried ice cream.

Later when Softi wanted a snack he opened the food storage locker and was surprised to find that all the ice cream was gone. That's strange, thought Softi. There are just a few crumbs left.

He didn't know that Eposh was snuggled up in a nearby cabinet, having a very nice time munching Softi's delicious ice cream.

After Softi landed the rocket next to the World Space Agency, he delivered his rock samples and Professor Puzzlepop was only too happy to give him a ride home. Softi didn't realize that Eposh was napping in his backpack.

When Softi stepped out of Professor Puzzlepop's helicopter, Tally and Robososfti ran out of the house to greet him. "Welcome home, space hamster," they shouted, and the three of them shared a big hug.

For the next few days the three friends played all their favorite games. Tally, Robosofti and Softi continued the soccer tournament that had been interrupted by the trip to space. Little did they know that someone wanted to join in.

Tally's mom had baked a big batch of chocolate chip cookies for Softi's homecoming. She had put them in the cookie jar. When Softi and Robosofti came in from the dining room after supper, the cookie jar was on the kitchen floor and cookies were scattered everywhere.

"What's going on?" Softi asked. "First my space ice cream disappears and now someone's been nibbling at the cookies."

Robosofti was just as puzzled as he was...until they saw a strange three-eyed creature gobbling down cookies as fast as he could get them into his mouth.

The next morning Tally went to wake up Softi and was very surprised to find Eposh snoring away. She shook him awake.

"Who are you and what are you?" she asked.

"I'm Eposh. I'm from Europa."

"You mean you followed Softi home?"

"Your Earth food is so yummy. I wanted to try more of it. We don't have anything like your crunchy circles back on Europa," said Eposh. "Cookies, Softi called them."

"No cookies?" asked Tally. "I wouldn't like that very much."

"Me either," said Softi, waking up and rubbing his eyes. "Good morning."

"Oh my gosh," said Tally, "I have to get going. It's almost time for school and I'm giving my presentation on space today." She put Softi and Eposh into her pockets and took them to school.

"Today my subject is space," Tally told the class. "We live in the Milky Way, which has a hundred billion stars. There are nine planets in our solar system. In space you can float because there's no gravity. As far as we know the only life in the galaxy is here on Earth. But I think if there was other life in the universe it would look like this model I've made."

She took Eposh out of her pocket and held him up on her palm. "Try not to move," she whispered to him.

Eposh winked at her and stayed very still. The class gathered around to see her alien. The kids thought it was very cool and the teacher gave her an A+.

When Tally, Softi and Eposh came home from school, they sat down with Robosofti and had a snack. Eposh thought that the mailbox key was fun to play with.

"Hey guys," Eposh said. "I'm sorry for eating your crinkly space food and crunchy circles."

"That's okay," said Softi. "I don't mind giving up my space ice cream and chocolate chip cookies if it means I can make a new friend."

"Maybe we should introduce Eposh to Professor Puzzlepop," said Tally. "He'd sure be interested to meet an alien.

"Good idea," said Robosofti.

The next day while Tally was in school Softi, Robosofti and Eposh went to Professor Puzzlepop's office. He was very excited to meet Eposh. The two liked each other instantly. There was so much the Professor wanted to learn from Eposh about life on Europa.

Eposh decided to stay at the World Space Agency as a super-special consultant, working with the Professor's research team on messages that would be sent out into space. The only thing he asked in return for his help was a big box of chocolate chip cookies every week.

Some weekends Eposh would go back to Tally's house to play soccer with his new friends. Other times Tally, Softi and Robosofti would spend the day with Eposh at Professor Puzzlepop's Observatory. Tally told the Professor that she wanted to be an astronaut when she grew up.

Whenever Tally, Softi and Robosofti visited the Observatory, they had a great time looking at the sky through a powerful telescope and talking about all the planets they hoped to visit one day.

"Wow! That telescope is amazing," said Tally.

"And so is Eposh," said Softi and Robosofti.

Lavinia's World is a company dedicated to children and to their families. Our aim is to teach children about the world around them and make learning fun. Proceeds from the sale of Lavinia's World products benefit children's causes.

Lavinia's World
titles available

The Little Stories of Manoosh and Baloosh

Make a Friend
Going Home
Bird Song

Softi's Adventures

The King of New York
Mission in Space
All Aboard!

The Kyss Family Mysteries

The Mystery of the Lost Bells
The Treasure of Lodian
The Great Paua Mystery

For a limited time only, collect all nine books, and send in proof of purchase seals with a return address to receive a free gift from Lavinia's World.
1100 Madison Avenue, Suite 3K-L, New York, New York 10028.
Visit our website for more information and fun stuff.
www.LaviniasWorld.com